OLIVIA
and the Haunted Hotel

adapted by Jodie Shepherd
based on the screenplay
"OLIVIA Plays Hotel"
written by Kate Boutilier and
Eryk Casemiro

illustrated by Patrick Spaziante

Simon Spotlight
New York   London   Toronto   Sydney

Based on the TV series *OLIVIA*™ as seen on Nickelodeon®

SIMON SPOTLIGHT
An imprint of Simon & Schuster Children's Publishing Division
1230 Avenue of the Americas, New York, New York 10020
For information about special discounts for bulk purchases, please contact Simon & Schuster Special Sales
at 1-866-506-1949 or business@simonandschuster.com.
Manufactured in the United States of America 0311 LAK 7 8 9 10
ISBN 978-1-4424-0182-2

"Look at all that rain!" exclaimed Olivia. "Thunder and lightning, too. I love spooky weather!"

"Did you have fun at school today?" asked Mother. Before anyone could answer there was an enormous *BOOM* of thunder.

Ian and Olivia yelled, "Wooohoo!"

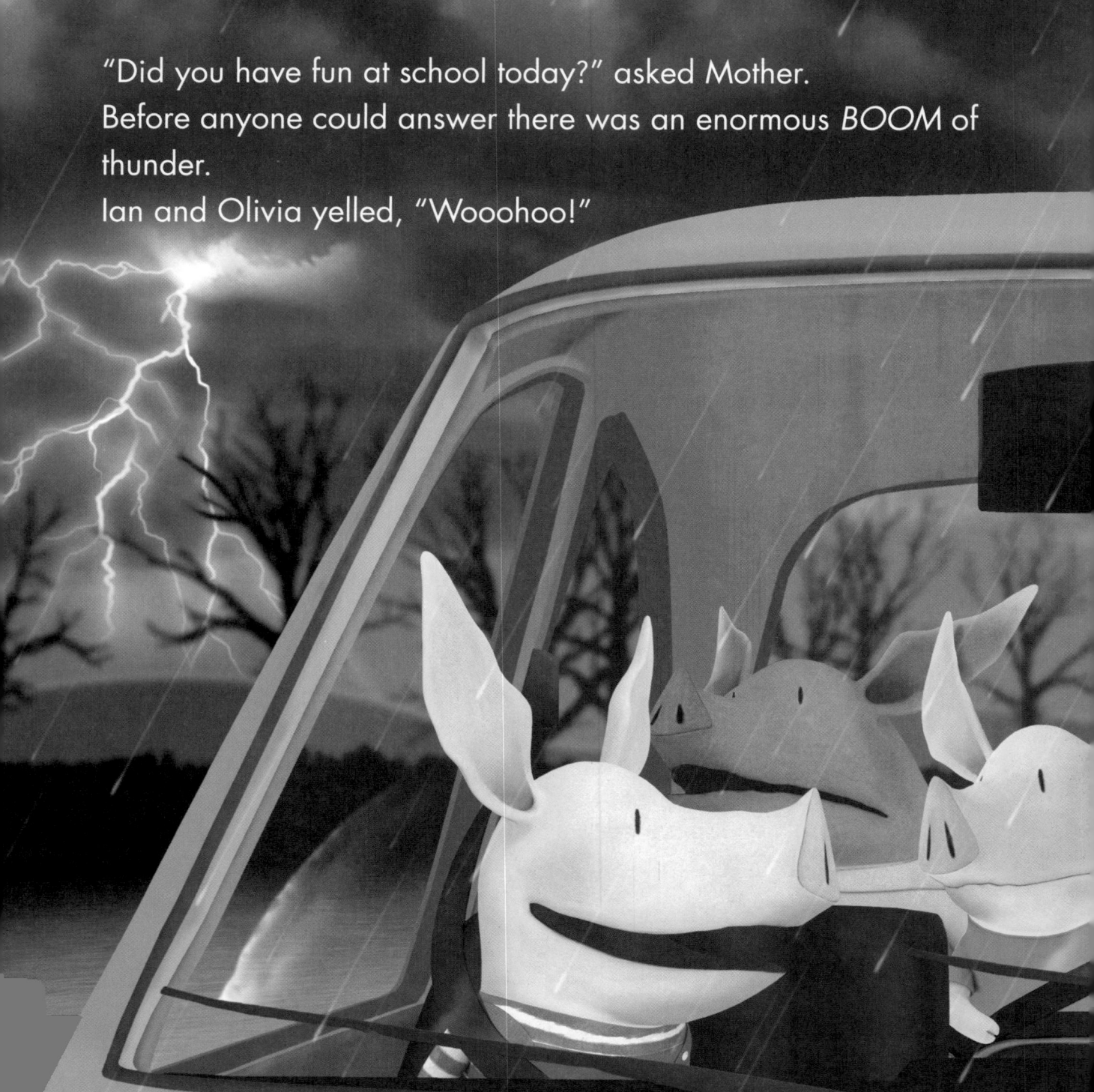

"I know the perfect game to play when we get to my house," said Olivia.

"Welcome to the Hotel Olivia," Olivia greets her guests.

"Please come in and make yourselves at home."

"Wow, it's so big!" Francine says.

"This is nothing," answers Olivia. "You should see my other hotels."

Olivia's house made a perfect hotel.

"I'd like a room, please," Francine requested.

"Me too," said Julian. "I mean a different room. Maybe one with a TV."

"Of course," Olivia replied politely. "That shouldn't be a problem."

There was a flash of lightning. *Whooo! Tap, tap, tap.*

The wind whistled and tree branches tapped on the windowpanes.

"What was that sound?" asked Julian nervously.

"Sounds like a ghost," Francine said, trembling.

"Ghost? The Hotel Olivia has no ghosts," Olivia answered firmly.

"Follow me, please."

"This is your room, Francine," said Olivia, opening a door.

"No offense, Olivia," said Francine, "but I'd like another room. This one smells like boy."

"I'll take it," said Julian. "I already smell like boy. Does it come with room service?"

"Of course," Olivia answered, opening the door to a second room. "All our rooms do. They also come with fluffy towels and chocolates on the pillows. That's what makes the Hotel Olivia the fanciest hotel in the world."

"I love my new room!" cried Francine. "This is the best hotel ever!"

Brring! A bell rang from downstairs.

"Excuse me," said Olivia. "I think I have another customer."

"I'm sorry, but the Hotel Olivia is completely full," Olivia told Ian.
"No fair," complained Ian. "Mom! Olivia says all the rooms in her hotel are taken."
"Olivia, I'm sure you can find a room for Ian *somewhere* in your large hotel," said Mother.

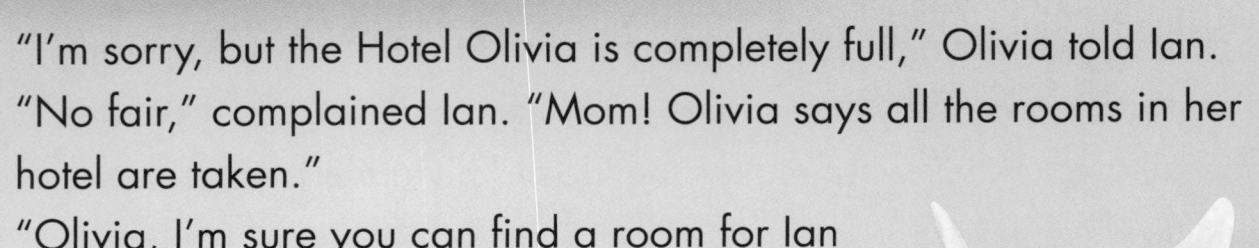

"This is our last room," Olivia announced. "You'll love the privacy. Plus the soaps are free. But you'll have to leave when the other guests need to use the bathroom."

"Never mind. I don't want to stay at this hotel anyway," said Ian. "Besides, I heard there were ghosts."

"Ghosts!" repeated Francine and Julian.

Room service kept Olivia very busy—too busy to play with her brother. She delivered lunches,

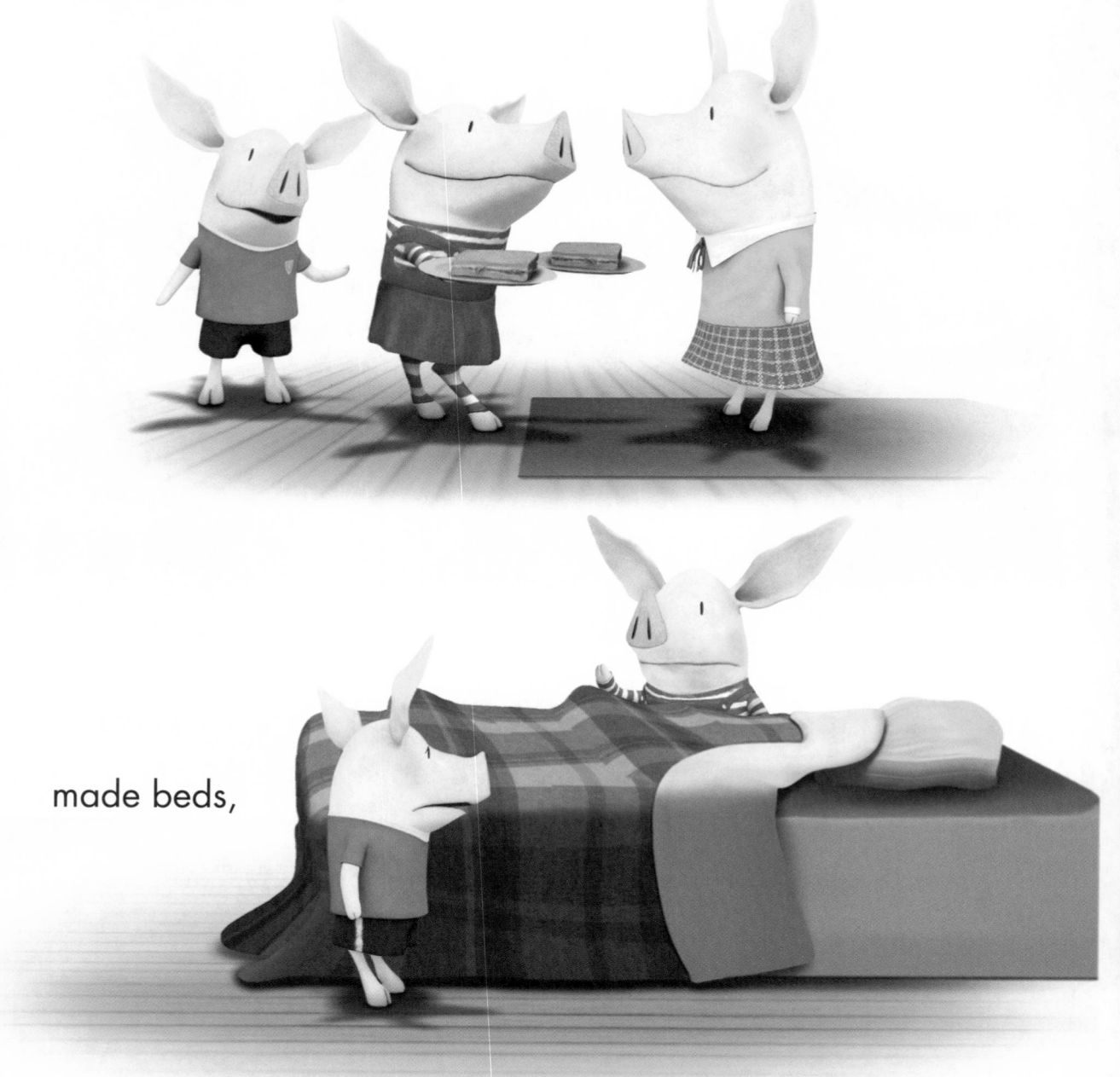

made beds,

cleaned up dog toys,

and soothed frightened guests.
"It's just the hotel laundry," reassured
Olivia.

That gave Ian an idea.

Suddenly there was a loud bang and everything went dark.
"HEY! WHO TURNED OUT THE LIGHTS?" yelled Francine, alarmed.
"The storm must have knocked the power out," guessed Julian.

"Or a ghost did,"
whispered Francine.
"I told you, Francine," said
Olivia, "there are no ghosts at
this hotel."

"BOO!"
"Aah! Ghost!" screamed Francine.
"Aah! I see it too!" screamed Julian.
"Where? There are no ghosts at the Hotel Olivia,"
Olivia repeated.

Francine and Julian huddled together. "Well, I saw a ghost," said Francine, "and I don't want to stay in this spooky hotel anymore." "Me neither," Julian agreed. "This hotel is haunted."

HMM. If I do have a ghost in my hotel, then I'm just going to have to get rid of it, Olivia thinks. Good thing I have a Ghost-o-Meter.

"I *knew* it was you, Ian!" said Olivia. Then she called downstairs.
"Mom, Ian is scaring my guests."
"Well, Olivia, maybe Ian just wants to play," Mother called back.
"Hmm," said Olivia. "I know! Ian, how would you like to be the
room-service waiter?"
"Cool!" said Ian.

"Welcome to breakfast at the ghost-free Hotel Olivia," said Ian the next morning. "Today we are serving our world-famous pancakes."

"Yum," said Francine.

"Double yum," said Julian.

"More pancakes, anyone?" asked Mother.

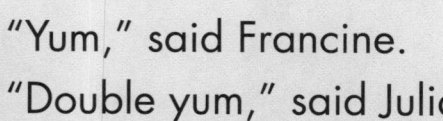

INDEX

B
birthday cards, 13
bullying, 13

C
chores, 9, 15
churches, 19

D
donations, 17, 19

F
feelings, 11, 21
food pantries, 17

H
hugs, 13

M
movies, 11

N
needs, 7, 17
neighbors, 15, 17

P
parents, 9, 11, 13, 17
pets, 15
plants, 19

R
reactions, 21
recycling, 19

S
schools, 13, 19
sharing, 9
shelter, 19
sickness, 5, 15

T
teasing, 13
"thank-you," 9

V
volunteers, 17

ABOUT THE AUTHOR

Lucia Raatma has written dozens of books for young readers. They are about famous people, historical events, ways to stay safe, and other topics. She lives in Florida's Tampa Bay area with her husband and their two children.

FIND OUT MORE

BOOKS

Cuyler, Margery. *Kindess Is Cooler, Mrs. Ruler.* New York: Simon and Schuster Children's Publishing, 2007.

Nettleton, Pamela Hill. *May I Help You? Kids Talk about Caring.* Minneapolis, MN: Picture Window Books, 2005.

WEB SITES

JustGive.org—Kids Corner
www.justgive.org/html/kidscorner/brandon.html
For a story about how one boy decided to make a difference in his community

JustGive.org—Ways to Give
www.justgive.org/html/ways/beagle.html
Read about how one girl helps keep her community clean

GLOSSARY

bully (BULL-ee) to scare or pick on people who are weaker than you

food pantry (FOOD PAN-tree) an organization that collects donations of food and then gives the food to people who are hungry and can't afford to buy it

planet (PLAN-it) one of the eight large heavenly bodies that circle the sun; Earth is a planet

recycling (ree-SYE-kling) processing old items so they can be used to make new products

shelter (SHEL-tur) a place where people or animals can stay to be safe and protected from danger

volunteer (vol-uhn-TIHR) to offer to do a job for no pay

When you are caring, you make other people feel special. They know that they are important to you. As you act in caring ways, you spread good feelings. Choose to do your part to make the world a more caring place.

Make a Guess!

What would happen if you were kind to everyone you saw? How do you think others would react? Try it! Hold the door open for someone. Wave to a small child. Pick up a bag that a shopper dropped. Did people react the way you thought they would?